George
B

ALLIES AND AXIS

George Birch

authorHOUSE®

AuthorHouse™ UK
1663 Liberty Drive
Bloomington, IN 47403 USA
www.authorhouse.co.uk
Phone: UK TFN: 0800 0148641 (Toll Free inside the UK)
*   UK Local: 02036 956322 (+44 20 3695 6322 from outside the UK)*

Published by AuthorHouse 07/09/2021

ISBN: 978-1-6655-9120-1 (sc)
ISBN: 978-1-6655-9119-5 (hc)
ISBN: 978-1-6655-9121-8 (e)

CONTENTS

CHAPTER 1

GOING TO WAR

"We are going to war," said John. "We have seen the propaganda posters really you guys. So, are we in hell? Yes. "We would like to join in the great war please." Oh you want to join the war in Europe and push the central powers back?"

"So, this is Europe not as I expected so you know. What are you doing?" said George.

"We are going to push the Germans back and maybe we could win this god dammed war," said George Harrington. Edward said, "It will be a long time till this war will be over. Hey, I am the king of Rome ha ha." As he was finishing, George cut him off. Because they were boys as young as 14, he did not want to frighten them. George said, "It will be a time that you haven't ever seen before." Then the boy named alexander asked how the war started.

He said, "Well, the Austro-Hungarian presumptive empire's emperor Franz Ferdinand was assassinated by a Serbian nationalist who shot him dead. Then Austria-Hungary declared war on Serbia and Russia declared war on Austria-Hungary. After that the Germans declared war on Russia. Then France declared war on Germany.

Then the Germans pushed through Belgium and that is why we are fighting this war. Italy stayed neutral during this war but now they have joined the war on our side. What about the east Lenin and the Bolsheviks? They took control of Russia or now it is called Union of Soviet Socialist Republics. Now it's 1917 and I do not know when it is going to be over.

Six months later

The Germans are still going through Reims and surrounded our forces. Then captured Paris right under our nose, so we made an army to counterattack their forces. Our General is a charismatic leader who will lead us to victory. His name is

Je André Ontrety et Lewis. He wears a fancy hat, a cloak and leather boots.

The General said, "Alright boys, this is the time we have been waiting for. Let's show the Germans our cold steel. Climb up out of the trench. Go! There are too many of them. We need to hold down the ground until our tanks come."

50 minutes later

"The tanks are here!" someone said. "Good!" General Lewis said. "Why did you call us?" a tank crew asked. The General responded, "Because I wanted to. We need you to push and smash through the enemies' lines." And we did. They will not get anywhere near Paris again.

CHAPTER 2

VERDUN

After we lost the first battle of Verdun, we won the battle of the Somme. We finally have a chance of pushing them back to the German border. And now we must take a stupid city called Chaumont. We lost 33,000 in the last battle. The Germans had lost 60,000. I will go home one day and see the county side and the peace we will have after the treaty is signed but we will not let the Germans push back. "So, you know the plan," said Edward. "First we need to take the city of Chaumont after we have taken the city, we march at Verdun."

Day one

"So, we need to take this city now so there will be no retreat!" "Yes sir!" "Climb out now" The machine gun open fire on the British and French soldiers. Even with the bombs that are exploding everywhere, Fred keeps going and we did it. We took the city. Now it is on to Verdun where we face the real German army lead by General Ludendorff. Men, we have come this far. We will not give up now chare!

"Hands up now!" said the German officer. We will give up now. Hi Ed, look! oh we found him. It's John. No! Why? This war has killed enough people. Now we are going to finish this for you John.

Two days later

Hi, where's John? He is dead. That is terrible! How did it happen? By a machine gun. They found him in a field near here. Do you know what is happening today? "No," said Edward. General Haig is inspiring his men with food, alcohol, and a speech. What for? Our major steppingstone to

Germany is Verdun. But what about all the deaths and for what major steppingstone? Oh shit, we're late. Come on!

Today men we fight a common enemy! And we know who is the imperial eagle, but they know that we are threatening to kill the iron eagle, so men stay strong and continue fighting this war!

How are you Edward Taylor? Good man! I am Bernard. Oh, I'm the boy you left on the field. Look I am sorry about that it's because the General said no retreat. It is all right! So what did you do before you joined this war? I was in school. WHAT? So, you left school to fight in a war? Yes, if I know what I was getting myself into this I wouldn't be here.

CHAPTER 3

THE END OF THE WAR

This is time we have been waiting for. We will have peace finally. It is about time now we take Europe from the Central Powers. The Ottoman empire has surrendered now. We have pushed them back all the way to Belgium's borders.

So, what's next? Brussels. WHAT! The Generals have decided on the attack. Why? It is very defenceless. It has been known that we are going to attack them and then this pathetic war will be over.

Look if we kill their officers, they will have no command so they will not know what they would do. We will pick the Germans off one by one. "Yes!" said Col. Sam.

Two hours later

Sir? What? They did it. Good! Go! Go! Go! Captain! What now? Look a light tank. Oh Jesus, they did not bring it to maintenance department. As the soldiers pass by, the light tank shot its gun and killed ten men. Look sir, there's a weak spot so if our artillery is shot, its back it will explode!

Well, yes! So you know what I am thinking. Oh, men get the artillery ready. Yes, sir! Hang on what are we firing at? THE TANK! You heard me. Fire now. As the shells came crashing down, it worked. "Yes," said Captain Sam. Go men!

We now push to a town hall. Damn it! What? They locked the door. Hey, give me that. What? Smash! Go in and find the General Ludendorff. As they run up the stairs, they found him. He was hiding. The Germans have surrendered to us. finally, we can go home.

Treaty of Versailles

CHAPTER 4

COMING HOME

So, we got on the boat and waved goodbye to mainland Europe. And we set sail to the British Isles. I can still remember all the things I saw and my friend John who is dead. But from all that, we will have a hero's welcome.

As he disembarks from the ship, Edward saw women and children clapping for their dad's son's brothers but even all that did not excuse the dead bodies that came to Britain. Then, he saw his family. He ran and hugged her. She wished he did not go at all. Then Sara said, "Where's john?" "He's dead." "What?" "Yes."

So, after ten days, he walked to his office. His job was businessman and turned politician. As he went in, he was greeted by his assistant James. He said you know that man named Mark is looking for you. "Why?" said Edward. He is in your office. Mark waves at Edward. Hi James, I'll see you at the King's Arm.

"So, what do you want?" said Edward. "Look, I have a deal for you," said Mark. "What is it? said Edward. I need some money. No, this conversation is over! Then Edward left immediately.

After that, he walked to the pub. The pub was called the King's Arms. He walked in and as he came, he was greeted by a man at first. He didn't know who he is but when he spoke, he said this, "Well, well, well look who it is!" It was the landlord. His name was Mike Henderson. Mike said, "How's the war?" It was terrible and I lost someone. Who? John. That's horrid! Anyway, what do you want to drink? Then James came. What took you… Mike! Oh yes. What did he want? Money. Why didn't he tell me? So, what are you having?

A beer please. One beer coming up. So you were in the war. You told me a little while. Yes, I fought at the Somme, Verdun, and Brussels. This is Matthew one of my closes friend. Matthew meet James good to see you! Ed had told me a lot about you. Really yes nothing bad. That's good.

Do you want? "Yes, sure. Why not wine? The landlord said, "Red or white?" Red please. I'll get it to you now. Good. Five minutes later, there you go pal! "Thanks," said Matthew. They talked. How's life treating you? It's good. "I can't complain," said Edward. How is work? It's good. Money is rolling in well. oh look at the time. "I need to go to the barbers," said Matthew. I need to go but we'll meet up tomorrow in the park.

So, then he went to the barbers. There was a queue. Oh crap! We are too late. How long will it be? I think two hours. Great! So what are we going to do for two hours? I spy with my little eye. I see something red. Is it a telephone box? No. Is it a post box? Yes. One hour later, hello sir, what can I do for you? I need a haircut. Okay, what kind of haircut do you want? Like my boss, Chamberlain. Okay. I'll get started right away. Thirty minutes later. How do I look? You look great! A strong leader like Chamberlain. "Thank you!", said Mathew.

He went back to his office. His business is car manufacturing and they are top of the line cars! Hello good morning Marian! Hi. What are you doing? I'm posting this letter. Oh ok. "Well, where's Edward?" said Matthew. I think he's gone to work. Thank you, so he went to Edwards's workplace. Matthew walked through the door and asked if Edward is there. "Yes," said his assistant. He's in his office. Hello Matthew! I would like a job please, but you are a dentist yes but no place to work in though.

So, can I have some money to get a building to start work in. okay look seeing that you are my friend I will give you some money for that okay so how much five hundred pounds. Fine hear you go I hope a cheque is fine yes. And I am finished there you go.

The next day Matthew came in and James his assistant said, "I remember you. You came in yesterday." Yes; I did. Is Edward in? No not yet. so what do you want I just want to tell him that bought a building were? Oh, just up the road. Okay, I must go to work now but you will tell him yes will. Hello sir, oh hi James what's is it a letter from who Matthew he just wanted to tell you that he has a found a building to do his work in.

That's good oh and he said that he will be in King's Arms pub. Three hours later, all right seeing we have no customers buying cars this afternoon, you can go home early. Do you mean it? Yes, so go. Oh James? Yes, Edward? Lock up for me.

"Will do sir," said James. I 'Il see you tomorrow, Good bye. So, after that he went to the pub.

Hey, I have been here for ages Edward. Wait a minute how long have you been here? Only thirty minutes. Shall we go in or are you waiting for someone else? No well go in then. Okay you first. Fine. Edward and Matthew went to the bar. "What are you having to drink," said Mike.

Two beers please. Here you go men. Thank you! Do you want to sit down? Yes, if you want. It is good to see you again James. So what do you want to drink? A gin. So…. but he was cut off by a man. Edward turned around and saw a man. This man looked familiar. His name is George Harrington. Well, well, well! Look who it is, Edward! Do you want a drink? A beer please. So, how long have you been friends? Since World War One. I met George in the trenches outside of Paris. I save him from the German machine gun, and I saw someone alive in no man land. So, I ran over the trench and nearly got shot but I saved the man. Then they took him to the infirmary. Two days later I went to the infirmary and I saw this man with a pen and book.

He was writing in a book when he saw me. He looked at me. That is an amazing story! Hey I'm getting a paper would anyone like anything? No thank you. A little bit later I've got a paper. Hey who's that? Adolf Hitler. This is a stupid question but have you meet him?

Yes, I was ordered to deliver a message from high command so I went across the land and saw a man I did not see before. He was trying to fix his bicycle. I slowly creeped up behind him to knock him out but I stepped on a stick. He got up and tried to shot me but I grabbed it out of his hand and he hit me in the face. I asked him his name and he said that his name is Adolf Hitler and he said, "Any last words?" Yes, you're are doing a terrible thing if you shoot me then you will die as well. What? There is a gunman in the tree line. So, he looked for the shooter. I got up and hit him in the head and ran off. Jesus and so that's why he has scar on his face. Well I'll be going now. Okay.

So, Edward and Matthew walked up the road when they got to the house. The house had lots of windows. There was a car outside, a union jack and a shed. The doors were big and wooden. They walked in the door. Oh hello, so this is where you live. Yes, this house was called the Taylor mansion. He lived with his wife Evie. So, I heard that you sent everybody home. Well, I must get ready for my meeting. I'll see you tomorrow okay. As he was waking to his workplace, he saw on a paper that Hitler won the election. Edward picked up the paper and read it. It says, "Today Germany has a new dictator. His name is Adolf Hitler, and he wants absolute power. This is threating the neighbouring countries." I fear that war will happen in Europe ...

CHAPTER 5

THE START OF WORLD WAR 2

War is happening again. Hey, do you want to join the war? Okay let's do that. Michael it is you who's enlisting, yes? You want to join hell? Yes. oh, look at that. What? Well, if you join you will be a General. Hang on, we will join. Well I salute to you General and Matthew. If I don't come back, then I have one request. What is it Edward? If my son come over from America, tell him that I am sorry. Now let's serve our country. These are your men General. They suitable to go to France. Today men most of you will die but our lives will not be in vain.

So as the boats went out to the ship, Edward, George, and Matthew waved goodbye to their family and friends again.

Come on men! March to the border of Belgium and stay there. Sir? Yes? Why are you not with the Generals? Why should I be there? Is there a war going on? Yes, of course. Why do you think we are here?

Then it happened. The artillery of the Nazis is bombarding us sir. Hold out. They'll stop. Thirty minutes later, they really have stopped. Good! Does that answer your question? "Yes, it does," said Matthew.

Hello General! What are you doing down here? They are my friends. Look if they want to stay with you can have them in rear command. My Colonel will find you accommodations here. Oh, and I nearly forgot. Forgot what? Some of your men will be going on an expedition. I'll tell you where tomorrow.

CHAPTER 6
DENMARK

What is the expedition? Where are we going? Denmark. There are important Nazi Generals that are meeting there. You are going to kill them. Okay sir! Your men will be sent on a transport ship to Denmark. Now that I've told you your mission, good luck! So, Matthew and George got on the ship. We are ready to go.

Two days later

Look sir? What? There's a blockade. "Oh shit can you go around?" said Matthew. No. Look, I'll drop you at a small village. What is it called is none of your concern. Matthew was a bit angry. They sided in the port Come out! Have we got everything on this expedition? There were ten men and all snipers. Lieutenant, what's the plan? We go up to the mountain and when it is dark, we move and when its light we sleep all the way to Copenhagen.

Then we kill all those Nazi Generals. So, have you got the rope? yes sir good get to it they tied the rope and started to clime when they were halfway?

So, Matthew keeps it steady hang on that's Hitler oh shit we cannot kill him out in the open but if he is on his own then take him out. George we are ready to shoot no we cannot why it is because there is a lot of Nazis down there so you Alexander you will go down there and kill Hansel and get out.

Alexander went down the mountain and saw Hansel went in a storage room. Alex saw a window and went through. It he was on the second floor and climbed down a ladder and saw the General Hansel and tried to slit his throat but when he tried to get out a German officer saw him and shot him, but he blew up the storage. Matthew and George saw it and said do not do it, but it was too late they misted.

The Germans had seen this they shot the two men then Matthew said we are going back now so they did but they were ambushed by a small force. Men get in! Cover now! Yes, sir. The force has beaten them, sir. Good! "How many died on our side," asked Matthew. "Two sir," said a soldier.

Well, we keep going. Okay. So they got the town. Oh, crap. They are looking for us. Come on! We sneak around then. As they were sneaking, they saw tons of soldiers up the mountain now. As they were climbing, the blizzard came and they could not be seen.

So, they got to the ship and ran for it, but Bock was running after him, but he couldn't get them. So, where to next? To France, I think. Edward needs a little chat.

CHAPTER 7

DUNKIRK

We are here. What a disaster then. Edward came up to Matthew and said I have a job for you. What is it now? You must radio British command. Oh, I'll do it. Good! So Edward, what are we going to do with the Germans? We will try to take the defences! We need to protect the soldiers that are going to escape to the boats and if any of the Nazis get through kill them. We must not let the Germans get to the beach.

Come here Matthew! They are in the houses you will take this sniper rifle and shoot them and if you see any divisions signal us. Yes, sir! Good. I must go to the ship. I'll wait for you. Watch out! As he was leaving, the Germans opened fire on small force. George, you're coming with me now. They started to climb and George said, "Have you got the sniper," Yes. Matthew shot the first one, but they stopped firing at the force and started firing at the house were Matthew and George was.

Then they saw him. It was Michael. He shot the remaining Nazis and he said, "Go to the beach. Edward will be there. Go! So, when they go to the beach it was like a massacre. There were dead men and they saw Edward on the ship. Edward said, "Come on." Wait, what about those that are injured?Leave them? No! So they got twenty injured men on the ship. And when they tried to get on the Germans came and said, "Stop right there you are under arrest. You are coming with us." So they followed the German officer and a bunch of guards who were taken as prisoners.

Meanwhile, General Taylor spoke to Edward. Hello Admiral. Edward said, "How is your fleet it?" It has seen better days." True but what will happen to the troops we left behind? I don't know. Most of them would be captured by the Germans. What have we done? We left our men to die.

CHAPTER 8

WELCOME TO EGYPT!

Hello, are you Edward? Yes. Who is asking It's General Montgomery! He is in the royal palace in Alexandria, I can take you if you want. Okay fine. As they were going to the palace, Edward saw dead bodies. Ed said, "Was there a fight here?" The courier said, "Yes, they have been trying to take the city."

We are here. Wow! This is extraordinary artwork. Come on. He will be waiting General Taylor. So, Edward you came? Yes sir. If you do not mind, what do you want from me? I'll tell you something. I want you to lead my army to take Libya. Okay sir. I will do it. Good man. We are not ready yet so where do I stay? Well, you can stay in the palace. This place has got a spare room. You can have. Thank you.

One month later after the French was kicked out of the mainland the Germans have been busy building a puppet called Vichy France. Also pearl harbour has been bombed by the Japanese so we have one ally more. But we are fighting in the Egyptian desert. I would like to be honest I wish we were fighting in Europe and Matthew and George is there.

But we need to take Africa at least I will not be in the fight. I will be pushing through the western Sahara to encircle Rommel's division while we are doing that General Montgomery will try to distract them. If you listen to our orders; we will bring you a victory.

Well General, when is the battle? Tomorrow. Good. Do you want to play twenty one? Okay. Edward looked at the cards and he had a jack, ace, queen that is better and I have twenty one. I'm the king of twenty one.

Lets see if that's true. Look at that! Jack, ace, queen ha in your face. You always win. "Wait, I have something up my sleeve," said Deric. I don't think you have met Debra, Jone, Molly and Victoria. Two queens and an ace. Well, you both got twenty one. You can split the money. Why do we always lose to them? Hey Admiral, it is not that bad. I think it is time to go to bed. Yes sir. We will have to get up for the battle tomorrow.

"The next day, men are you ready? Yes, then get in your tanks and kill those Nazis now!" Edward said. Goooo! They went to the tanks and get ready to attack.

We are ready to push through the western Sahara and take out rommel's forces then Montgomery will attack the South of of Libya and then we push through the the north and encircle him so the artillery rained down around around the sky and destroyed all types of Panzer divisions who were standing in their way. Men what should we do now? We push through the lines and then we take him out. Holy shamoly! The Germans have got some big guns. We need to take them out before anything else. If they destroy Montgomery army then we will be crippled out here so if you have a chance destroy it. Yes Sir! said the soldiers.

Meanwhile in the South, Montgomery was having some trouble. "Where are those reinforcements?" he said. A soldier replied, "We don't know Sir but I think that they have been taken as prisoners or killed. Then we'll be out here and they'll have a clear route to Alexandria. If that happens we will be sieged in this city. Over in Edwards team, what is happening out there? "They are firing shells sir," said a soldier. Look sir. We can see it. See what? The artillery gun. Well, shoot it then they shot at it. It went up in flames and that is what we call a masterpiece now we need to get to Montgomery so we can aid him to take the city of Annacrack.

So, they came on the battlefield and saw all the tanks that are destroyed. Most of them were German but it still a loss of life. The allied armies charged into the city centre and raise the flag of Great Britain. Well well well, General Taylor you have exceeded all my expectations.

I have to congratulate you. If we didn't have your planning then we would have probably lost this battle. So where to now? The German still occupy a lot of the French territory. This is just one of many battles and then we don't know. We don't plan the wars that we are in. We take them one step at a time. Thank you.

So man it's time for what to take the Tunisian Fort this is the last major area that the Germans own so we will attack them at night when they are asleep and raise the flag of the French they'll surrender and Rommel will be kicked out of Africa but what about Algeria and all the other places the

French and the on the US is going to try and do that but what did they fail they won't I know it General Julio is a powerful General and let his men into battle numerous times so you don't have anything to worry about that's good so as we were going in through the sewers we saw rats but we found the manhole to climb out of we grabbed a Nazi officer and killed him in the sewers so we creeped around gums loaded if you see anyone kill if they Nazis.

So we climbed up a hill And saw a car coming towards us we hid in the Bush but it went past and then we got to the gate a soldier said we can't go through there why because it's locked hang on.

I'll shoot it why it'll notify the guards not my gum it has a special modifier on it it's silent then shoot it edward shot the gate and went in show men shut up and be quiet and they raised the flag of the French but the soldiers came out and siad hands up no it is your hands what should be up and then they came crashing in and said you are now a prisoner give up now are you will die fine siad the Nazi officer.

CHAPTER 9

IMPRISONED

I woke up in the dark and dingy cell. There was a man in front of the cell. But then the cell door opened and a man came in and said wake up wake up! Matthew said, "No!" Then soldier got him up. He dragged Matthew up and hit him in the face. Ow! You are coming with us. "Why?" said Matthew. Because I said so. Now come. As they were walking down the corridor, Matthew saw prisoners in their cells. One prisoner said, "What are you staring at? Do you want to fight with me?" "No," said Matthew. So they walked straight to the courtyard then the cells open.

The men came out were prisoners. They said you have

enough time to get some exercise and food. So then Matthew and George went in the dinner hall and saw the food.

That's it. Yes. Set the dinner man. So Matthew and George sat down. They met a man who had no legs and he said look I know how to get out of here. The warden has a key it can fit any lock. So how do we get it? He often carries it around with him but he goes to solitary confinement a lot so if you got locked up there, you'll be able to get it.

And how do I get there well a fight will do it look you have to beat up about 3 or 4 a couple of them will only amuse the guards and what about when I'm in there you normally goes towards you pickpocket him.

Then come back to me and then you can be on your way to work I presume back to England why there the only place where the Nazis haven't taken yet and we are still loyal to our country.

Then Matthew and George went up to the baddest people ever and said you guys suck what siad the first man you know what I'm talking about you're going down as the first man fell to the ground the second man came in he said I'll teach you some manners buck George punched him right in the mouth and in the balls he also said.

The second one went to the ground I will beat you up, said the third one, but it didn't In fact, the soldier broke it up he said you two are coming with us where to consolidari confinement. Now you know the plan take the key yes siad matthew you are all a bunch of dogs so I think a bit more solitaire confinement will cool you down. He turned his back the warden and Matthew quickly grabbed the key and got his batton and hit him and choked him to death were then he unlocked the door and opened the door were George was in come on as they went past they we're almost caught almost see by Nazi Sergeant that was close let's go they find the door and went through it.

Good work! Now go fine aren't you not going with us I'll just be a waste anyway you are freedom i don't I'm from Poland doesn't exist and I can't walk remember Oh yeah see ya goodbye friend be good knowing you fine we were getting out of that place so we went out the front door dressed up as Nazis we went to the car and stopped near a train track and said george they'll be waking up soon we best not wait around. So how do we go home by that train come on come on quickly quickly so as they were running they climbed on the back of the train.

Oh that was hard but now we're on then the Nazi General Gavarian siad keep moving you fools yes Sir they opened fire on the back of the train but it was too late Sir eight other prisoners have escaped what why was I not informed they've escaped by your warden he's dead blast.

Haha we'll be seeing you over the channel you inbred idiots Sir should I call the SS I'll call them you get all the rest here and have them executed for what has happened here we cannot have no more prisoners will save it there will be a there was a riot find 20 of your troops but you're terrible at their job yes Sir I know the people for it well I would like you to kill them for me why though because then it will look realistic and why should we do this siad franze because then they'll think that we were overrun and we couldn't really keep them of course I will find them one day they've escaped me once they've tried to kill me once they were the same people in Copenhagen but their luck is running out.

The next day they asked Colonel Hila so when General Gavarian arrives what should we say that we were overrun when you looked out the window there was dead bodies good. sorry General it's good to see you at last you came all this way to tell me that you have missed me no Sir I won't waste your time for that good now what about these prisoners would have escaped escaped no no no they have not escaped we were out numbered by 10 men I believe no no no this was a full scale riot hm it is very interesting that I know it is but this is very strange times we are living in after all we are at war again.

May I see the bodies of course Jesus it was a bloodbath in the there was bodies everywhere and this place won't was are courtyard this is where they first strike well you wanted to see us where is the Walden he's dead and you have let a bunch of war criminals free in France well done Colonel you are a disgrace to the riek yes Sir and if anything like this happens again I will not hesitate I'm killing you I'm not making myself clear yes Sir very good now go on back to your work of course.

Matthew my feet are aching can we not just stay in that cottage for a bit are you kidding me will be court for sure oh find so Matthew and George walked all the way down to the streams of Normandy where they will get a boat hey Mr hello do you know any boat rides to the channel no sadly not after them Germans confiscated my ship and when I got it back it's in tatters.

How am I gonna sail up? What do you need? Iron for a start. Let me see, some paint as well. Is that it? No need to fix the artillery piece on the front last been out to date since early 1930s Il see what can be done you know you're a real man you are I know weres some iron it's in a convoy I've seen a couple go past they try and sell me stuff but I've seen some iron so if you can take them out bring me the iron and some paint it's all in that convoy how many soldiers are we expecting 20 or 30 I don't know but get it and I will get you over the channel thanks.

So as George Matthew we're going to the rendezvous point where we will pick off every single one of the Nazis is anyone got any problems with that play saying it like that there's only me said George fine don't get in my way we came all this way together I think you can treat me with some respect find men fire Bang Bang good job let's go go go get in George bang he shot a man in the chest why then he died they drove it as quick as they can and lost them down a ditch they came out and they said to the captain of the ship is your supplies good good but the ship won't be ready yet So what the hell do we do look you can lay on the low at my house okay and then once you finished grab as much things as you can carry and then torched the place Now how long will it take couple of days no more than three great.

Three days later

Well we must burn the place grab as much as you can the started hoarding everything into bags and other things that's good let's go they lit the candle and through it on the floor Are you ready I've been ready since day one to get out of this place did.

You burn me house down yeah great let's go as they were going through the channel race of ships until one persons head Sir what set the first mate German ships that's the Bismarck what the hell is the best mark it's the new German battleship we can't take that down Sir British ships on the port bow it's the hood is the admiralship they won't sink that well it doesn't matter go now and so sprung into action Jesus the waves are rocky today 8 weeks later land ahoy the white cliffs of Dover where is saved yeah as they were coming into port the captain said where's my payment hey you go £15 cheers Sir bless ye.

In the end the British did sink the Bismarck I'm pretty much backing the British Navy and the saying goes rule Britannia and this could alter the war forever.

CHAPTER 10

THE SHIP IS YOURS NOW

As we got out of the ship there were tonnes of soldiers and ships in the harbour but Matthew saw a man who look familiar to them and they knew who. It's Edward Taylor their General friend. He came to get more resources for the war in Africa against the Germans so they went to him and said "hello I don't believe it," he replied. How did you escape? Someone helped us get away. Was it a guard? No. A prisoner then? Yes, he had no legs and this is why you are in England. Yeah and you wanna still fight? Of course. You do want to serve our country proud. Well look, I'm not supposed to do this but you have been through a lot and so I'll make you Matthew a captain and you George a Colonel. Thank you it's an honour to fight for the King's army.

Do you see that British flag? Yeah, I see it. That's what we're fighting for...for freedom. Never forget that. I wont. So, will you come with us to Africa? Yes, I don't know. You can get on that big ship. I'll let you have it really and it's mine forever as long as you like. How can I refuse? Well, then welcome aboard captain. Shall we set sail? Sure why not.

Three days later

Sir Sir wake up oh what happened said Matthew he passed out Sir so we brought you to your cabin it's not bad could do a bit more paint though can't complain looks at what in the fog is that ships so far east especially if they are German captain you best look at this what is it now holy hell who's done this it's burning Sir ship Hoy three German ships Jesus they're on the attack they know that losing in in Africa they turned around and was ready to fight them but after the blue Admiral Cunningham fleet arrived and sunk every single one of them that it go back to the mainland where you belong.

Show Admiral why are you here because I need to talk

to you what is it now look we are helping the Americans to push back the Japanese why do I care the Japanese are very powerful and if they take over we'll lose parts of our empire and it will be hard to take it back we need to protect India if we lose India they'll have a good attack at our African colonies okay will do it keep going we're at the port sir there is a change of plan.

We're not landing here we're sailing to midway oh you've got to be kidding me as we were sailing to the Indian Ocean we saw a blockade Matthew said what should we do about the blockade we need to take it out now OK Sir fire up as the ships collided to each other the crew opened fire on the Japanese kill em all any of these idiots going back to the mainland yes captain storms brewing crap is the guns ready yes fire they shot the hull and it exploded good job said Edward what should we do now we need to destroy the other two Sir you best look at this holy hell that's the American Navy.

Good job Americans hey it looks like there Navy is better the what it was in World War One cause it is we've always fixed ours up since the war so they fix this I get it but you know well they need to protect their mainland oh why would they even have it I agree.

Hello, my name is Douglas MacArthur. Ah so you're here to help the governor? No and what will happen I've told you well they've taken the defences but the governor is in India Today Governor Hutchinson I believe yes it is how do you even know him because the prisoner told me about him in the fortress he said that he knew him I say so can I see him alright so are you getting ready for the Battle of Midway said the American soldier yeah well only do every single ship to take out the Japanese. Look if we can take out their entire Navy here we can finally attack their divisions in the South and push them back watch me the taking French indochina that taken of Malaya Hong Kong Singapore an over known territories and north Borneo yes but if we can do this we can land troops at the strategic bases and then we can cripple him from the winning the war against the Japanese well you must know what you're doing course I do so how long will this take.

It will take too long for us to build up our new Navy how many were sunk while you were here we came with time we we have no eight ships good for the amerucans then we have over 15 ships to be sent here but four was sunk so you have 11 left so the rest of the fleet will be going to the Battle of Midway only two will be staying here okay we well

Be preparing for the battle these are the plans what I've got let's see him hey there yes I can because I've got a great plan and the plan everyone will need to carry out this will alter the war for us do not let Douglas McCarthy down do not let General Taylor down and do not let our democracies fall to the Nazis at the Japanese because remember the Japanese are a dangerous race and they will destroy anything what gets in their way state motto is not to protect that civilian's their motto is the honourable thing is to die in battle and the most not loyal thing to do is to live and betray the Japanese empire I know I know but we will give our allies Toms materials for fixing our country those countries will not fall under a Nazi regime will not fall under and Japanese regime and will not fall by an Italian regime that is why you are fighting that is what Douglas McCarthy said make us proud.

CHAPTER 11

BATTLE OF MIDWAY

So when we got there the Japanese were losing General McCarthy led four carriers and 16 battleships and 32 schooner's whilst the British had seven carriers and 32 battleships so when we got that we fired at the Japanese schooner's. The battle was about to begin with Matthew ship. Edward said keep going but then they saw more ships. We will be unstoppable said Edward. You know the plan. We need to keep going and keep as many ships as alive as we can. It would be impossible for the Japanese to send their ships and then send their kamikaze planes to blow us up with.

So we heard the screams of the sailors and then I saw a giant ship it was the best Japanese torpedo that they have ever had and Edward said it's coming towards us Bryce everybody it hit the side of the ship Admiral are you alright yes he replied let's Jacamo who he's the best Admiral of the imperial Japanese empire theres ships are coming out of the fog he's trying to destroy us find him and kill him.

Yes Sir they went through and saw his ship it was dumped it was a super battleship we opened fire on it as hard as we could it took half an hour but their guns were out of Commission good get us alongside of the ship and I will kill Jacamo as Matthew and George climbed onto the ship they heard two guards saying that hey Jacamo is in the control tower five soldiers around him you can't get up there unless you got clearance some people I well he is the best Amaral that we've got I know that they climbed up the ladder and saw an officer with with a card and Matthew said hey look he's got a key card so George grabbed him from behind and strangled him and then took his uniform knowing that he couldn't speak any Japanese. George would have to rely on saying that he lost his voice or his tongue.

As he was walking up to the control tower he saw two guards outside he said to him are you alright he lost his tongue where are you from in Japanese of course German we're famous Generals and we want to pay a visit to him as you wish go ahead the Japanese guard opened the door and there he was Jacamo then he turned around and said well well well you too I don't know you well you probably will Matthew pulled out his gun but then he turned around too quickly I need grab that gun out of his hand I then hey got the catana and started fighting with him Matthew also grabbed a sword from a Japanese officer and started to fight he kept on fighting until he kicked him and then he got a knife from his pocket and then stabbed him in his stomach and he said oh why did you do this to me what reason did you give Matthew replied you were killing innocent people we did the best thing that what could be done but these people they were living in ignorance and we showed them the key to the cage I am just a puppet of my master and you think that my plan is not already in power you think that you are better than us cause you're wield your blade and you gun and you will never as a take us down again so you think that it's right to kill innocent civilians the civilian's have done nothing very did what had to be done for the people these people deserve to die not cause they wanted to I did this high cost greatness in my people.

People will remember them as their Admiral, great leader,

emperor and hero too. They will not be so kind to my death and do you think that just because you're better than all of us?

You have these kind of people as well. Like your Prime Minister for example. Winston Churchill is nothing more than a bully. He has murdered innocent Africans and Asian people. He has killed the people who desired to freely govern themselves. Now, they don't have the chance to do that. So, we will find you all and we will kill you in your sleep, ha ha. What else should I say Admiral? Everything I had have been taken away from me already.

"You spin a tale for what you have done Jacamo but we know that you are an evil man not as much as Hitler. Be that as it may you are still bad. What I did is for my country. Did we do terrible things? Yes we did but we did great things too. But you, everything that you do is a monstrosity. Jackie Mel may you rest in peace now," said Matthew.

Now it is time to go to back to africia.

CHAPTER 12

RETURN TO AFRICA

So this is Africa. I thought it was going to be a lot more sandy because you're in the capital of Egypt. Edward thank God I found you Montgomery what are you doing here I thought you went to the Middle East to fight those vishis and the Germans I was sent back here Rommel is planning another attack they've been kicked out of abyssinia Somalia and then Eritrea so they want us to take Libya we took half of that we just need to find.

Sir! Sir! what is it now Jake Rommel is not leading it who is it then some Italian called daborga he's one of the best General they've ever had how good is it you pushed us out of Somaliland and even threatened parts of some of the hardest areas to take So what are we doing we need to kill him what where are we even gonna find him.

Okay so he's in a fort. so how do we get in there I have a tank I've been waiting for a special mission like this so you can use it Matthew yeah have you ever wanted to drive a tank course I've always wanted to do that well I need you to occupy as many of those Germans and their battalions as much as you can course I'll try my best and then when you're in the for you'll find him in his quarters but this man has one weakness and what's that that is too cautious he didn't attack in World War One because he was scared that they would attack them first so we'll just overpowering if we can take him by surprise he'll send most of his divisions out and il try and escape that's why you are going to light the fortress on fire to make him think that we have got a bigger army then his so as we were going through the darkness Matthew said can we have a rest okay they rested for two hours and continued to drive watch out boys we are deep in Italian territory it was 4:00 o'clock in the morning and we fired the shots but the Italian tanks look out more of them the Germans are trying 2 keep there man in cheque take him out as they were loading the gun they shot at the German tanks.

Good Sir we have a problem what is it it won't start try and fix it it won't help hang on the tank how we gonna destroy that it looks like the last one hang on all to it said George go as he ran he saw his entire life flash in front of them put it through looking aid in it as he went down by machine gunfire he said now go how did you talk me into this help go go never mind about me just one thing don't spare kill him no no Matthew started to cry then Edwards said come on we need to go in.

Hey look are you gonna help us wow if we help them they could start a riot it but first I would need to get some arms where's the armoury down there Mr hey good as they went down there was an Italian sleeping they hit him on the head and he was knocked out they looked around and saw tonnes of guns so they picked up about 20 and carried him to them to the prisoners Are you ready to call some trouble obviously I am Good then commended officer said charge so they started there riot Sir being attacked what find the rest of these idiots them send them out Edward can you hold this line sure why not what am I gonna do you find the borgia.

The battle was brutal keep fighting are you captain Maxwell yeah who's asking we were in the battle remember oh the person I sent to Montgomery watch out stopped a German captain in the face keep fighting man another one stabbed through an Italian soldiers throat oh how disgusting look it's war fire men shoot them good job three bombers they started to bomb the fortress look there is an anti air gun come on they pushed 2 Italian soldiers off the bridge and they went crashing down and died come on get on fire and then they shot the engine and he went down into a building the other two went away yes.

Meanwhile Matthew went in the side door and came in he saw no one so we opened the door and there he was borgia so you're here to kill me like what you did to Jacamo then get it over with Matthew slitch the knife across his throat he was bleeding out and then Matthew said do you have anything to say.

Do you think I'm scared off a little pup I am the best Italian General well if they agree to you just because you're good at fighting I was very good at strategy but you were weak I was not weak I am the best what Mussolini has ever had in his regiment and that is why I am chief of staff and you are just a stupid Colonel and you stink but I am not as great as you think that I am all this time you've never learned anything you're the evil one we are the bring us a piece Italy Germany and Japan will all be together and a country if we don't have power then we will fail as a country and you think that I am one of the best you were thinking that I was going to be Rommel he's gone to Paris you will never ever find him again Oh yes we will I just want to tell you something wall you don't have a clue but what Rommel is doing is going to kill the chief of staff he thinks that he is a weak man he is the only person who does not agree with Hitler and his crew but he was an amazing General before the Nazis came to power I know that he is a noble man he is he didn't want this war but we don't have a choice of wars he can't tell him nothing you think everything Rommel wants to be chief of staff so it can be the new leader he wants to kill him he wants power and I gave him power.

By giving him power to my leaders that's why he's so evil what do you see out there a glorious empire what I say is weak dictators how dare you we are your betters yall no one please he he tried stop Mussolini and gvarian wanted to stop Hitler they controls us we don't want to do this but you had the choice to rebel do you not see what would happen to us have you not seen the Jews murdered in the camps it's horrible the

German empire was evil but they are a different type of evil they didn't listen we have a lessened and now we have paid the price off sons dying how family members dying in this stupid war but they still think that we are winning just one thing I just want to say I'm sorry for theblood shed okay and then he died he said to Edward he's dead job I know it was hard but it deserted you've done it for George.

CHAPTER 13

BEFORE D-DAY

Ha good job let's get to the ship now damn it is on fire look for some planes let's take them are they British cause they are will get in as they flow across the continent they saw Spain from above they flew over France and saw camps being built in the region then Edward said hey is that the place where you were held no their concentration camps what are they for Jews Muslims people who aren't really loyal to the Reich we need to stop them before they do anymore well it's a well they've lost some of their best Generals I don't think they're going to be such a big problem.

Look a runway the two landed on the runway a pilot came to him and said oh we were thinking that you were a concentrate team no what happened to we just heard on the German radio but they have sunk a German ship but the main pilot fluitt into the ship he kamikazed into the ship said Edward but it's terrible at well anyway what are you doing here we were trapped in after him yeah I heard about daborgia.

So what do you want you don't know who I am my name is General Taylor ah you're here to meet General Eisenhower yeah I am well he's gonna plan to defeat the Germans or going to land what we can't tell you why because the spies everywhere all over this country now so it's an invasion in France good I'll see him immediately.

A ship slided into port and then Matthew said hey that's my ship this is not your ship anymore you stole my vessels fighters we can protect our Navy so it's just been sunk every single time maybe you should have it looked after that's what we were going to do before they were stolen here is your fighters so you're gonna find some new ships for us.

No I'm not I'll tell General Eisenhower this five will find you some ships how many do you need we need 11 ships 11 then the big trading port in Liverpool where you can go of course course we gotta go there fine we'll go ah General my name is Edward James yes Edward do you know your way around Liverpool of course where I was born where I used to live there so you can find this little place where is it's a trading port used by the British Navy why do you want this for a fleet we need 11 ships we can just buy them no I am not using my money for ships what will be sunk quite right look I am General okay yes we know so we drove and drove through the countryside until we got to Liverpool were there was lots of people where is the port down this road and then turn left and then go forward then turn left okay thanks we got out of the car and started to walk the city with a lot more power than what I've been through said Edward not as nice as Manchester have to agree let's go so they continue to walk and walk and walk then they saw the port there were ships crew members an merchants all selling and buying there goods where is the Admiral he's gone to the pub so Edward walked to the pub with Matthew they entered and there he was drinking away then Matthew said look we need your fleet the man replied I give it to you if if I outdrink you'll let us have the fleet.

Good luck with that you can't do that touch I'm better go and get the beers Edward sorry General Taylor that's better as the first pint went down their throats they felt nothing boat when they got onto the 7th and 8th they were pretty much hammered Oh my head but eight one the man had passed out on the ground we've won this was worth it.

Oh the next day they threw a bucket of water all over the Admiral a want you do that sober you up Oh no drunk again don't worry you weren't the only one I had to throw is why I was already is awake I just did it was fun shut up said Matthew now you have to agreed to the bet what was the bet again you give us 11 ships and two cruises and one carrier and we won't tell the Admiral staff okay I can give you 11 ships one cruiser and that's were they shock hands with Edward good now he's got the ships let's go.

They came back and he said you got it all done then I I won't tell anyone about this good Oh yeah General Eisenhower wants to see you as well that's what I was doing before well very sorry but thank you how have more ships now we only had sex you could assess yeah but now we have more ships than what we could ever hope for yeah great.

Where the hell have you two been look up caught up into something well you've heard that we're gonna attack France we know a perfect plan we are going to attack in Normandy well then we storm the beaches pushed through Brittany take Paris and then we've taken France back from those Nazis but after that you will have to kill Rommel and Gavarian and then when we still not we push into Belgium the Rhine Luxembourg the Netherlands and then we've won the war over about Italy Italy has sadly collapsed and the regime went out fighting there and if we win then it'll be a bloody war for the world but what if we can't win the the Germans are dwindling everywhere I think we can win but what about the Japanese on the left after you killed Jacamo the Navy is not as powerful as Britons or the US's so we've beat them remember most there are empire is naval like Indonesia I love the islands as well I say we understand good great get prepared do whatever you need to do and then will be setting off everything okay great.

CHAPTER 14

D-DAY

So are you going on the landing ships course we are when is it gonna happen about 6:30 okay but won't we have to send paratroopers and of course we will be how by sky and then it's the landings Matthew yes you're very good on your feet then you will be going over in France why we need someone to die I will not die okay good so Matthew walked out and there he was the pilot the pilot said hey are you the person they're gonna send out yeah so what are we gonna do I've never done this before. Well I fly you under you jump out we survive and will be decorated as heroes yeah show me where Come on when you landed cut down some communications and other things okay as they flew over Matthew jumped out of the door.

The next day, look Sir those transports are coming towards us a German soldier said look Rommel well anyway let's go as they ran on the beaches they saw Americans and their allies being murdered on the beach keep your head down and you won't be shot men yes General.

That machine gun recking us Matthew I knew that you wasn't gonna die anyway we can talk about this later I need you to take this grenade and blow that bunker out the retreat and then we'll take the beaches so as Matthew was moving around he saw some guard he opened fire onto and shot one of them the other one ran he didn't care to kill that one.

Look there it is get it there we go I've done it General it blew up and as they predicted they retreated the German officer said come on back back the men pushed them back.

Sir the beaches are ours how many did we lose not a lot 15,000 15 grand the terrible thing they won't forget this but we will beat Hitler we've beat Italy they can't keep these lands anymore even the Nazis own high ranking Generals can't even win.

Two weeks later we're finally ready to go to Paris and

take that and liberate friends but we know there is two major Generals though who is it Rommel and Gavarian.

Boom what was that it's a tank so are we going to destroy that thing I don't know give me the Panzer shred he shot it and it destroyed the tank good shot thank you.

What are you waiting for climb up now hang on before you go what's the plan they'll be in the notradam that's what our spy say you need to go through the mountains okay then it's plain sailing but not so easy like that but I think we can do good.

CHAPTER 15

THE END OF GAVARIAN AND ROMMEL

As they enter parish Matthew said services Paris is bigger than I expected be quiet okay Edward sorry General so what's the plan set Matthew okay get to notradam then when we are there there will be a side door and walk through it hide behind something and then we take him out with a silenced pistols okay but before we could do that we need to take out the snipers there on that roof that roof and that one so I'll just go Yep and don't get cold.

As he was climbing up the ladder he grabbed a German foot I pushed him off the edge next one Edward strangled to death and the left one ran off well all the soldiers where killed I know we are going in the church and finally killing gvarian.

Get here now the probability of two Generals in the same place to die we can't kill him yet why not because we won't be able to know what they talking about this could be a plan it's to easy to kill then now the must be a plan behind this talking about I don't know hang on.

Hiel Hitler Rommel said so you know the plan no we must try and push the allies out of France again how do we do that I am leaving this area and we're going back to Germany why because we are doomed here we're not doomed we are holding the allies at the strategic points we have a new plan what is it is to do an intense fire bombing campaign I also use some of the Japanese tactics what tactics have you ever heard of kamikazes no what's then you fly the plane to the ground they blow up and kill tonnes of soldiers that is our plan and what if the plan fails then we will be doomed in this hellhole France isn't that bad then a German soldier came in with a prisoner look what I found a lurking around the streets trying to escape from us oh was it who are you captain sparkle Roman hit him in the face and he said you're gonna tell me now you're just gonna kill me anyway so why should I tell you anything haha you'll never win one we.

I've had enough so Rommel pulled the trigger on his gun

and killed the pilot who flew Matthew in is that of course he is you want to say the same fate don't be smart with me how do I made myself clear yes Sir good.

But then when they turned around Rommel pulled out his gun so did gvarian and then they shot each other and then gvarian siad why because you were making Hitler weak come on we need to go now why the dead is not something that we wanted no we didn't want gvarian to die come on we need to get out of Paris now look they're gonna burn down notradam no not this time so as they were moving it Edward just as a Nazi officer and shot it it exploded and killed 50 of the soldiers he changed into his outfit and they ran off as quick as they can well we've saved the national landmark. Well I better be going now.

Why now? so they got in the car and drove all the way back hello General Taylor hello Colonel have you done that thing of mine yeah but sadly gvarian dead he was the enemy yes but he didn't deserve to die like that did you kill him no Rommel did and gvarian shot him.

Where are you going to Paris seriously yeah shall we replenish our horses we've already done that they practised that kamikazes on some of our trading routes we should wait no we will not wait for some stupid trade routes we are going to keep marching General Patton I don't think you don't know the plan that we are prepared to do General Montgomery is going to March South and see if he can beat up he's a weak and entitled fool who can't do a simple task.

He is one of our best Generals would I tell you that Douglas McCarthy is bad and all he wants is power and victory. He does not care about his soldiers well. Guess what I know that you're lying to me because he is one of the greatest victors in this country he is liberating Europe from the Nazis regime we allies in this war not a bunch of squabbling countries but what if we can't win failing in the east the West and in Italy they will collapse even their regime is falling around them left riots are ensuring all over the cities even Hitler knows that she's failed. He's not failed he's still very powerful I know that's why we're going to arrest him how do you know other days even gonna cooperate he will have a death sentence anyway.

So we'll march to Paris immediately well that defence is down well they're not prepared to destroy their own city seriously yeah we saw him torching not to damn so we need to push very hard through Paris and then we've taking the city France will be liberated and then it's Belgium then when we've taken that next every Germany and then we'll kill Hitler I may have a little surprise for the Japanese but we'll talk about that a later time.

CHAPTER 16

BATTLE OF PARIS

Keep fighting men who breakdown line soon enough what's happening they are retreating something happened General yes what is it General Taylors army has pushed north now and is threatening the heart of the city we can't have any Nazis destroying this city yes we will try now that the Gavarian's death the German army is not very strong he was the only one who was rather keeping the army together another in shambles set up the machine gun fire down 30 troops good job we need to keep moving hold the town square we keep moving.

Look General the shooting from the buildings fire fire we need to kill every single one of these Germans the trying to distract us they know they're on the run Edward pulled out his gun but before we could shoot a man came out he had a shotgun and shot the german soldier in the head who are you he was French I am Lewis for two years these people have tried to kill us I know it's time for us to rebel and out of nowhere 50 other revolutionaries went into the streets and started to riot this gave him a good distraction thanks Lewis.

Don't mention it well done I think we can go hang on before you go we can hold him out for as long as you want will send two divisions down here to kill them you just try and get in there alive okay I'll do that.

Men what's happening now we've met heavy resistance we need to keep pushing no we need to push back no we hold this line now we don't retreat until we upper purred to retreat look we're so close to victory do not forget what you are fighting for his right a man said.

Come on put this British flag up now we've done it Sir I know retreating back were to now to the next target natra damn but first of all we need someone to go in there where in the palace it's a cathedral no we need you to destroy that tanks easy just plant these explosives and then press the button then they will blow up so now we gotta do then we take in Paris but it won't be that easy you're gonna take about ten soldiers captain my name is captain Rogers or Elliot of course will go on as they were walking down the road they saw tanks hold up why are we stopping said Matthew look at that Barb wire tanks and all sorts of things.

So have you got a plan yeah so someone go next to the tank and shoot him then climb into the tank and destroy the engine send it then we'll take the rest out there's only one tank there such as destroy okay they ran out and then Elliott said fire men fire the guns were opening fire on the division then Matthew went into the tank shot the driver blew the tank up and the rest was gunned down.

How did that go smooth enough you know thank God we're not dead Colonel captain what is it it seems that the Germans have left all the city we found the only 2000 peoples the left of the Germans most of them must have been retreating well anyway they've all gone to Germany I see.

Good job I have to congratulate you have done well well now Paris is ours now to Belgium and then Germany.

CHAPTER 17

THE BATTLE OF BELGIUM AND LUXEMBOURG

After France was liberated the Germans have became a lot more aggressive now they have new tigers and panzers they're supposed to stop us from invade Luxembourg and Belgium from the Germans but we are led by a good General General Patton I know he's a bit stubborn at times but at least he's for he said if we invade Belgium Luxembourg and then Netherlands once we have done that we will be able to parse towards Germany Hitler he is losing influence all over the rike and they know this that's why they're trying to stop us put that failing.

So the first squad will be attacking Luxembourg and the second squad will be attacking Belgium once luxembourg's force has done that they encircled the German forces and take them out then the left to push back to Germany it's quite smart I notice.

Are you ready to destroy some weak Germans yeah thank you.

As on the battlefield I saw panzers hey hey Edward do you know the planet yes tank divisions need to be destroyed before they can March of course we need to destroy some of the fences OK but don't destroy any of the buildings yes we won't good.

So you have a telegram what is it it's to tell them that they have already taken Luxembourg what General Finns he's planning something he knows our encirclement movement So what will happen well will have to try and take Brussels now it will be impossible to take the city what we need to try or thousands of peoples lives will be at stake you're right man which charging in so as they were charging those hardly nobody left was left of their army was really aterrible army was left behind and they had done it they took the Netherlands Belgium and Luxembourg no the Belgian was taken.

Hey Edward yes Matthew what is it Churchill is doing a speech on the radio wait we have a radio yeah we found it in the office that's a German radio no Williams got it working that is good.

In 1940, we were pushed out of Europe by the Nazi but no we are pushing them abck. People we must continue to fight for this country. We must continue to provide for our country. This country is not a slave anymore. I have faught for you in our darkest times. Hand our greatest victory we are not fallen out so this war it's coming to an end.

Well we are the beacon on the hill. They say that we are amazing and our courageous and brave soldiers has made our country greater than what it has ever become if we had Neville Chamberlain or George banks elected we would not do as well. Neville Chamberlain was a good leader, he tried and tried to get peace in Europe but Hitler back to no avail. Why are we fighting in this horrific war for domination? All because of one man. Do not forget that one thing in this country and it is freedom. Freedom of choice and freedom of speech which should be under true power but for democracy This is why you are fighting for this war. Remember a man is not born a monster but bullying and other cruel things that has happened to him. Look at what he has done he was manipulated by his uncle and his mother that was Winston Churchill. Thank you! War is really over. Hitler won't be able to survive this cable. Good job just remember what Churchill said.

CHAPTER 18

THE FALL OF NAZI GERMANY

Germany collapsed. They lost the war. The Germans we're very angry after losing Frankfurt. The German people had given up on the German Reich. This was really the end of Germany. Hitler knew this. It couldn't keep going. The Germans continued to be pushed back and continued and continued and continued.

They tried to put up a last stand here at the battle of Saxony. All atrocities were made but they know that it was over. Hitler was escorted down to the bunker with the rest of his Generals and then it happened Hitler committed suicide and all his best Generals as well. This man had tried but failed.

The Soviets in Berlin tried to find Hitler but he was dead. News went around the world and people started to wave flags around. Churchill was celebrating saying that they had defeated a common enemy and now peace was in that country the treaty was signed.

CHAPTER 19

A BOMB BABY

So when we came on the boat. They said, "Are you ready?" and then we saw it it was horrifying so many have died to this atomic bomb. No we have radiated the water system and food and then Edward said "My God what have we done to Hashima and Nagasaki ? Well they're just being flattened. We have became a death bringer."

After the US dropped the nuclear bombs, Japan surrendered. War was finally over or was it? In the rubble of chaos two rival factions with two different ideologies would start a different war called the Cold War.

Through the rubbles of World War One and Two you will follow these men Edward, Matthew and George and other ones as well with their tragic life story going through war and prosecution. Then seeing a complete nuclear atomic annihilation.

Buckle up and enjoy the war.